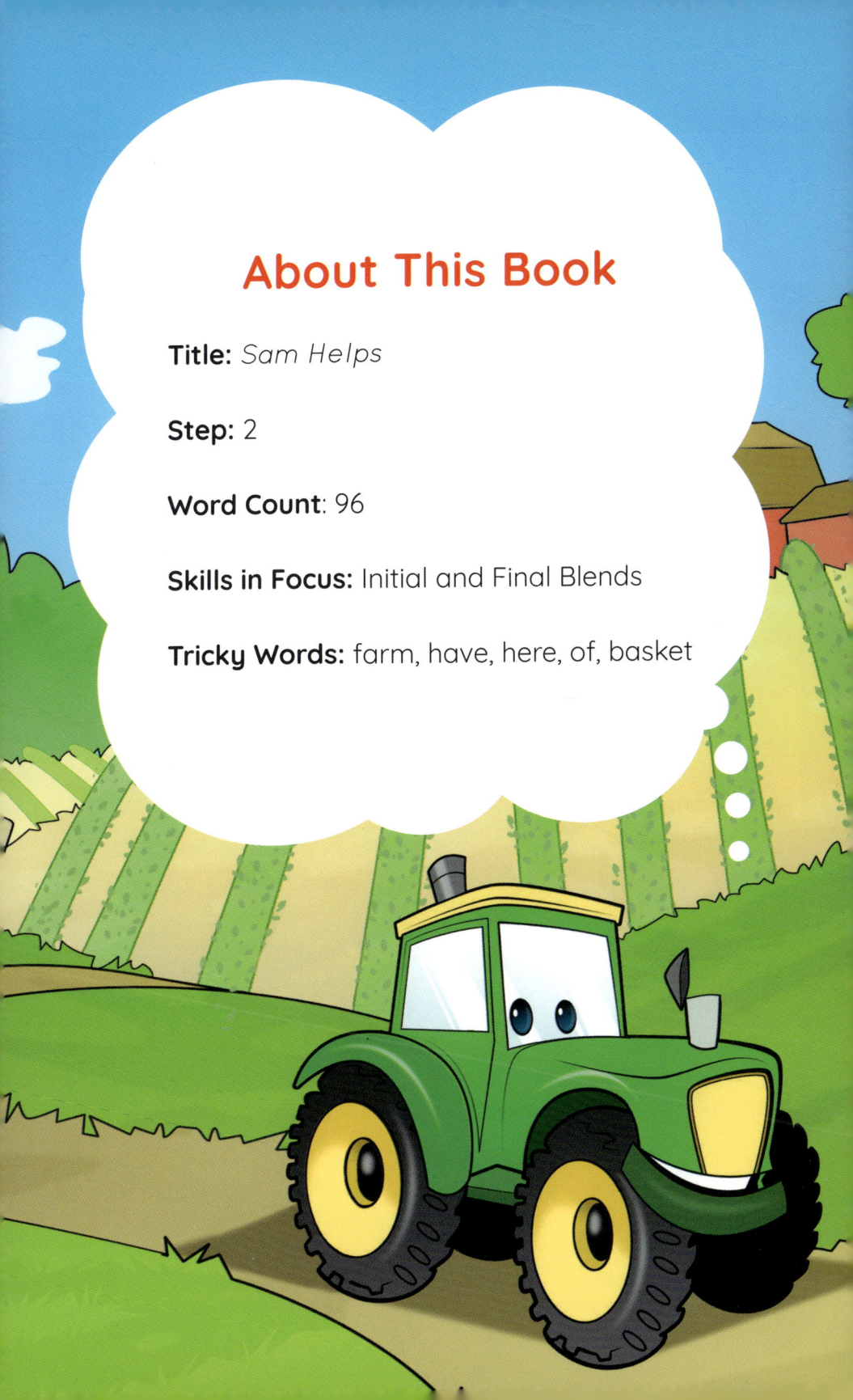

About This Book

Title: *Sam Helps*

Step: 2

Word Count: 96

Skills in Focus: Initial and Final Blends

Tricky Words: farm, have, here, of, basket

Ideas for Using this Book

Before Reading:
- **Comprehension:** Look at the title and cover image together. Ask the reader to make a prediction.
- **Accuracy:** Practice the tricky words listed on Page 1.
- **Phonemic Awareness:** Explain to the reader that a blend is two consonants together that each make a sound. Discuss that blends can be at the beginning of a word or at the end of a word. Preview story words containing blends, beginning with *help*. Segment the sounds slowly and have the students call out the word. Offer other examples that will appear in the book: *lend, dust*. Call attention to each blend and where it is found within the word.

During Reading:
- Have the reader point under each word as they read it.
- **Decoding:** If stuck on a word, help readers say each sound and blend it together smoothly.
- **Comprehension:** Invite students to add to or change their prediction from before reading.

After Reading:
Discuss the book. Some ideas for questions:
- Who are the characters in the story? Who is the main character?
- Describe the setting.
- What problem did Sam face in the end? How did his pals help him solve the problem?

Gus, Sam, Jen, and Tim are pals.

Sam's plants are here, but Sam is not.

Sam has to get to his job.

Sam gets set to help on the farm.

Sam can help till the land.

Sam can pull baskets of yams.

Sam is spent. Sam is a mess!

Sam is back. Sam has a lot of mud and dust on him!

Can Sam's pals help him?

"I bet Jen can help him," Gus tells Tim.

"I can help Sam!" yells Jen.

Sam is glad to have pals.

More Ideas:

Phonemic Awareness Activity

Practicing Initial and Final Blends:
Tell readers they will segment the sounds of story words containing a blend. Provide a ball for the student to bounce each time they segment and make a sound. Call attention to the blend in each word.

Optional: Snap, clap, or tap the word if a ball isn't available.

Suggested words: *plant, play, lend, tend, hand, land, rest, dust*

Extended Learning Activity

Beginning-Middle-End:
Sam spends a full day helping at the farm. Provide the reader with a three-box organizer labeled "Beginning/Middle/End." Have the students retell the story by drawing three events that took place throughout Sam's day. Then, use the illustrations to orally retell the story.

Optional: Challenge readers to label their pictures.

Published by Picture Window Books,
an imprint of Capstone
1710 Roe Crest Drive,
North Mankato, Minnesota 56003
capstonepub.com

Sam Helps was originally published as
Helpful Tractor, copyright 2012 Stone Arch Books.

Copyright © 2024 by Capstone.
All rights reserved. No part of this publication may be reproduced in whole or in part, or stored in a retrieval system, or transmitted in any form or by any means, electronic, mechanical, photocopying, recording, or otherwise, without written permission of the publisher.

Library of Congress Cataloging-in-Publication Data is available on the Library of Congress website.

ISBN: 9780756594886 (hardback)
ISBN: 9780756583859 (paperback)
ISBN: 9780756583835 (eBook PDF)

Printed and bound in the USA. 5757